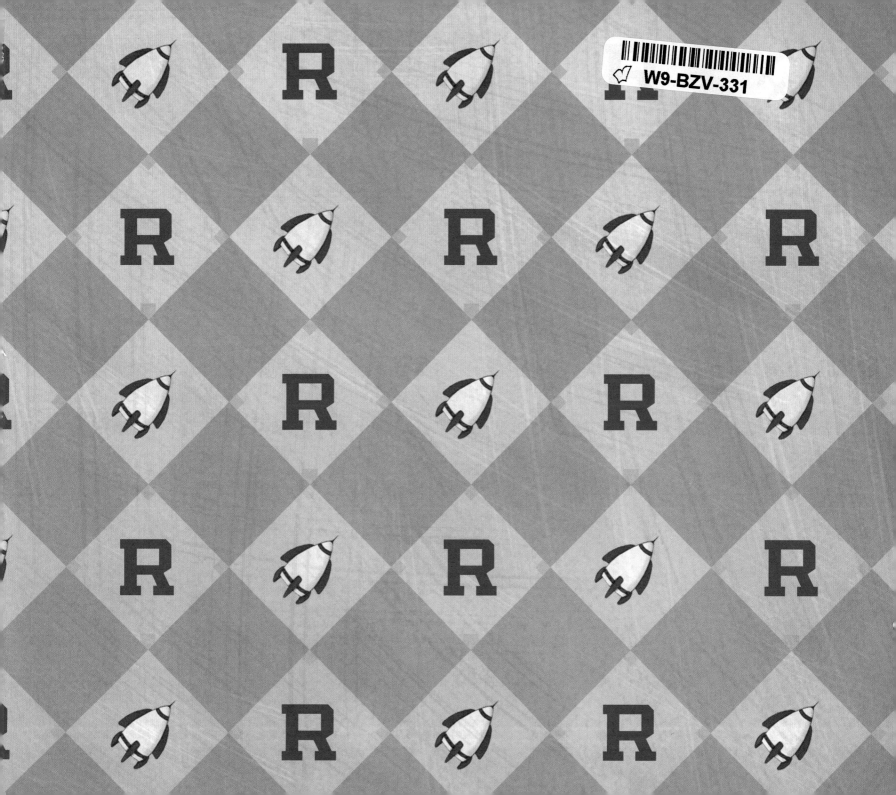

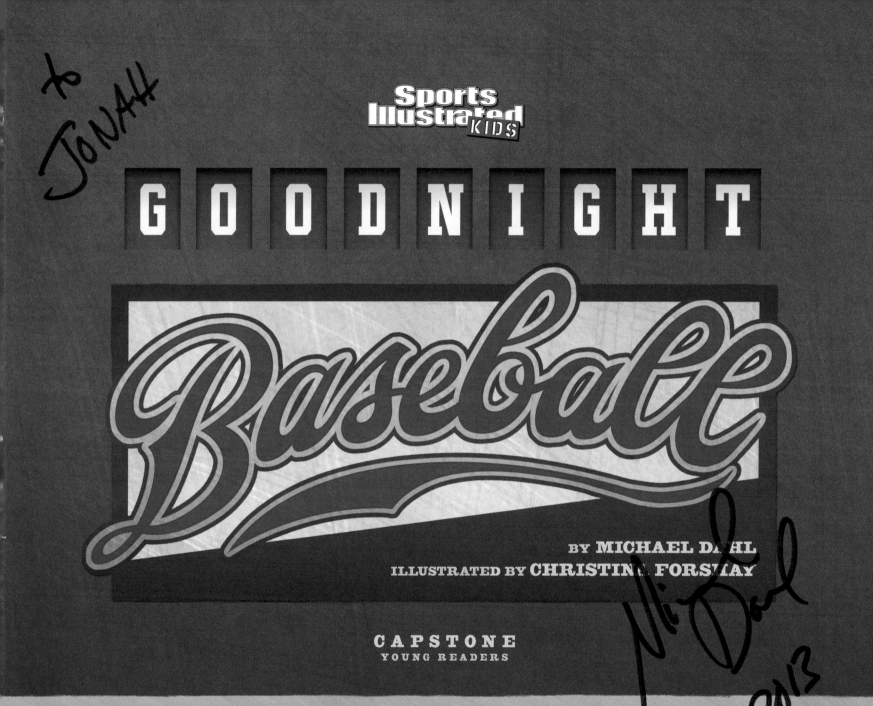

Sports Illustrated KIDS

GOODNIGHT

Baseball

BY MICHAEL DAHL

ILLUSTRATED BY CHRISTINA FORSHAY

CAPSTONE
YOUNG READERS

to Jonah

Michael Dahl

2013

The great big stadium is outside of town.

Fans and friends come
from miles around.

We walk through the gates.

We each take our places . . .

To get a good view of the
mound and the bases.

We eat popcorn and hot dogs
and hold drinks in our laps . . .

with the names of
our favorite teams
bright on our caps.

We watch all the players
who catch and who throw,

and the runners who race
to each base down below.

WOW!

Then, the crack of a bat —
A home run!
What a hit!

Look! The little ball lands in one lucky fan's mitt!

The fans stand and stretch at the late seventh inning.

And the game goes on, the home team close to winning.

Everyone cheers. The home team won!

Now the fans are all chanting, "We're number one!"

Then the crowd waves goodbye.

Goodnight, teams.

VICTORY!

You played a great game!
Now sleep well, and sweet dreams.

Goodnight, diamond.

Goodnight, grass.

Goodnight, home plate
where each runner ran past.

Goodnight, bat.

GO ROC

Goodnight, mitt

that reached up high and caught a fast hit.

Goodnight, popcorn boxes under the stands.

Goodnight, mascot and goodnight, fans!

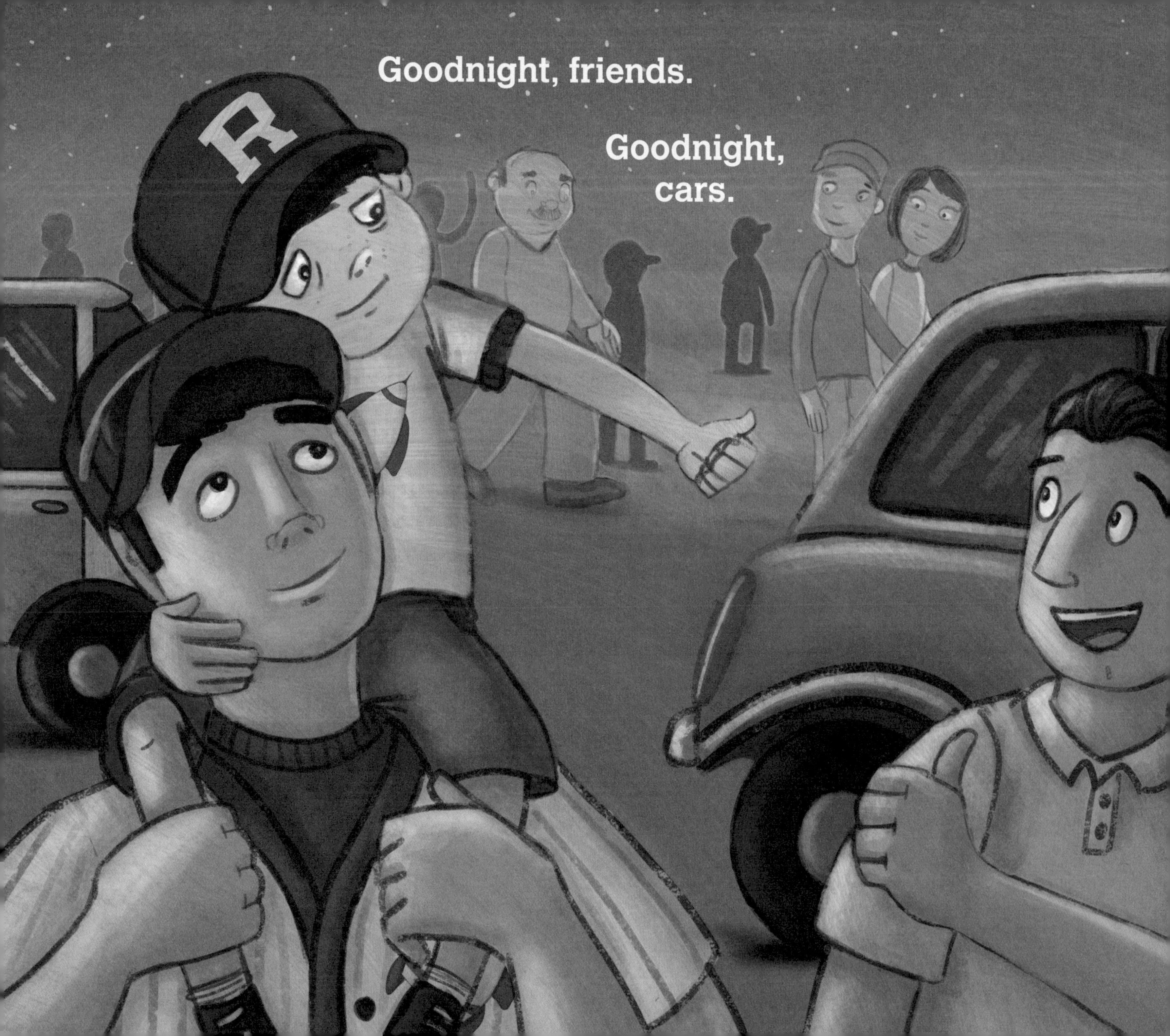

Goodnight, friends.

Goodnight, cars.

Goodnight, stadium, under the stars..

Goodnight,
Daddy.

Goodnight, moon.

Goodnight, baseball,
safe in my room.

Published by

CAPSTONE YOUNG READERS

a Capstone imprint

1710 Roe Crest Drive, North Mankato, Minnesota 56003

www.capstoneyoungreaders.com

Library of Congress Cataloging-in-Publication data is
available on the Library of Congress website.

ISBN: 978-1-62370-000-3 (hardcover)
ISBN: 978-1-4048-7979-9 (library binding)

Designer: Bob Lentz

Printed in the United States of America in Stevens Point, Wisconsin.
042013   007298R